MY CAUTIOUS BOSS

Office Affairs

Amy Thompson

About the author

Bestselling author Amy Thompson writes short, exciting, sweet romances. Of course, no romance story is complete without a strong, ALPHA MALE who can't live without her and will do anything he can to keep a smile on his queen's face. Sit back, put yourself in a comfortable place, and dive into sweet romantic happily ever after stories.

Table of Contents

Chapter 1

Lydia

"I still can't believe you're making acting a part-time job, Lydia," Gracie says with a little frown on her face as I continue to tie the laces of my sneakers. Gracie is my cousin and my roommate. We've been living together for five full years. I am only a year older than her, but she acts like she is my aunt or my mother. She is a trained teacher, who teaches in one of the best schools in town, and maybe that's why she treats me like I'm one of her students.

I'm beginning my job as a personal trainer in the best gym in town today, and I am so excited about eventually pursuing my career. Since I was ten, I have always wished to work in a gym and own one; therefore, I learned all it takes to be a trainer, and I am now certified. I'm twenty-six now, and I'll be starting my first gym work today.

Talk of acting; I went into acting because my father wanted me to. I enjoy acting too, but not as much as I am going to enjoy my new work at the gym. Jasmine, one of the actresses I work with, told the owner of the gym about me, and he said I could start work today. We will be meeting each other for the first time today.

I feel a tap on my shoulder.

"You still have to explain why you're making acting your second choice," Gracie asks while I try to avoid her questioning look.

"Acting has never been a second choice, and I think you understand that already," I reply, looking into the mirror to see if I am good to go. This is my first time, and I have to look so good for everyone. If there is anything I won't joke with- it is my dress. Of course, I have to dress like a sports star all through, but I will do my best to look gorgeous.

Gracie moves close to me and repacks my hair into a smooth ponytail.

"You know that, whatever choice you make, I'll always be on your side. I see you have passion for this, and I can't stop you, can I?" Gracie says calmly. I give her a smile, turn to her, and plant a kiss on her forehead. Gracie can be crazy at times, but she really loves me.

"Thank you, Gracie."

"Don't be late. Since it's your first time at work, I'm going to make something delicious for you before you leave."

I rush out of the house, get in my car, and drive straight to ERA gym. I pull my car to a halt as soon as I get to the park, hop out of my car, and head straight to the building.

"Hi, I'm Lydia, and I'm here to see Mr. Martins."

"Oh! Tell me you're the new trainer," says the old security man standing right before me.

I am so surprised right now that the security man knows about me already. I thought I would have to explain myself to him if he asked about my mission.

"I am," I respond with a smile on my face as he leads me to an office in the gym.

We enter, and I see a gorgeous man sitting on one of the luxurious office chairs: he must be the boss. His handsome face makes me nervous. I don't know how tall he is because he is on a seat, but I am very sure he is tall and well-built.

He has dark hair and pink sexy lips that make my mind wander. He is on a call, and I watch every move of his lips. He beckons at me to sit on one of the chairs before him while the security man leaves. I try to control myself and of course prevent my eyes from looking at those sexy lips of his, but I just can't- my mouth is so hungry for them, but I don't think that will be possible.

"I'm so sorry for keeping you waiting," he says after dropping the call. "You are?"

"Lydia Staples," I reply.

"Okay, and you're here for?"

Confusion begins to run through my mind. Why did he ask like he is just hearing about me? Jasmine had called him right in my presence, and I spoke to him over the phone.

"I'm from Jasmine Tate and-"

He interrupts me. "Oh, I remember now. You're the new trainer."

"Yeah." I nod.

"I'm Eric Martins, and I'm the humble owner of this place. I'm also the operations manager," he introduces. "Let me call one of the staff to put you through. I'm quite busy right now."

I nod as he places a call through to a lady who enters and leads me out of the office to show me around the gym and everything I need to know.

Eric

The beautiful new face that left my office earlier keeps flashing through my mind, and I feel like seeing her again. I had totally forgotten that I was expecting a new trainer. Since my wife died, my mind has been drifting apart.

My wife died a month ago- she died of cancer. I loved her and don't think I'm going to love any other woman in my life, but seeing the exposed cleavage of the young lady that just left my office caused arousal in my pants, and I think I want a woman again. I haven't had sex since my wife's death and have not felt such arousal since her death like I felt earlier. A few minutes earlier while she was right before me, I felt like grabbing her and making her feel the arousal she caused, but that would be too funny. She is my employee anyways. She is mine now: I'm the boss here.

I hear a knock on the door.

"Come in, please."

Steve enters. Steve is my childhood friend and my bestie. We discuss almost everything. He has been visiting regularly since I lost my wife and does everything to get me out of my thoughts.

"What's up, man," I greet.

"You want to know what's up?" Steve asks. "There's a hot chic right in this building."

"Who? One of the customers?" I ask innocently.

"Don't tell me you don't know that your new employee is hot."

I roll my eyes and sigh. "Really? So you know I have a new employee?"

"Of course, yes. I made an inquiry already."

"Good. So what's with her?"

"Nothing, she's sexy, and I'm only trying to remind you of the great beauty breathing underneath your roof."

It is true. Lydia is sexy, and no man would dispute that fact. Hearing more about Lydia's beauty from my own friend makes me yearn for her more.

Steve winks at me to draw me out of my thoughts. "You can grab your copy before someone else takes charge."

I know what Steve is talking about, and this is not the first time he will be making such a suggestion. Ever since

Emerald's death, Steve had wanted me to go out on a date with another woman just to get over everything.

"See, Steve, I don't think I'm ready to do this now. My wife-"

"Oh! Come on. She is no longer your wife! She is gone and gone forever, and you should move on with your life."

I change the topic and let Emerald and Lydia's topic go for that moment.

Chapter 2

Lydia

"Bend this way, then begin to twist that waist slowly," I say to the five old men standing before me, struggling with the moves I gave them. Eric is standing right behind the old men, watching my moves and theirs with his arms folded.

"Now I need you all to split those legs, this way," I say as I show them what they are supposed to do. Eric stands watching. Now his eyes are fixed on me- on my ass. I smile as I realize that.

It's been two weeks since I started my work here at the gym, and my feelings for Eric grow so wild that I want every part of him day by day. I had gone to his office a week earlier, and I had seductively looked at him. Not that I planned to but because he stared at my shirt's opened button. I thought I completed all the buttons, but I missed one of them, and my boss saw a part of my breast. As soon as I realized he was staring at my tits, I winked at him.

Eric

I am staring at her ass right now. She is damn hot, and I can't resist that any longer. The way she twists her waist gets my mind wandering off to bed with her. It'd been a long time since I had sex, and I think I need to right now. I unfold my arms and place a finger on my lips to carefully access her every move. I can't wait to get my dick into her hole. My friend had told me to grab my copy, and that's exactly what I'm going to do. A week earlier, I had seen part of her tits. They look so fresh, plump and innocent. I just can't wait to fondle them and deprive them of their innocence.

She is done with training, and I beckon at her to see me in my office. I move to my office while I wait for her patiently. A few minutes after, she enters with a smile on her face and gets herself comfortable on the chair before I could tell her to.

"Yeah, I'm here, boss."

I love the fact that she calls me *boss*. It makes me feel like I own every single part of her. No one calls me *boss* in this place except Lydia. I don't know why she calls me that, but I sure know she is handling a great responsibility over to me.

"Good job out there. How many old folks do we have here?"

"Ten of them," she replies.

The question I asked wasn't necessary, but I just need a conversation to come up.

"I need you to come over to my place tomorrow morning. I think I need some exercise," I say, looking straight into her sexy eyes.

"But, I have to resume work as early as six tomorrow. I don't want to miss it," she replies.

I nod in agreement. "Yeah, I know you have to resume work as early as possible tomorrow, but I insist you come over to my place tomorrow morning. If it is about here, I'm going to send someone over to train your students, while you come over to my place to train me."

"Okay, so what time do I resume at your place?"

"As early as 5:30 a.m. or maybe 6:00a.m," I say, handing her a card that has my residential address.

"Okay."

"Yeah, so I will see you tomorrow morning," I remind her.

"Sure. I have to leave now. The next session starts now," she says, standing up while I permit her to. I watch as she leaves the office. Her ass calls to me for help as she sways out of my office. I am not so sure I am taking the right step. My wife's death is still fresh, and I'm not supposed to be flirting with other women.

The news about my wife's death did not go so well on me. I had just finished at the gym when I was called by the doctor that I had lost her. While Emerald was alive, I loved her with everything, and I never cheated on her. *What will the press say?* - That I lost my wife a month ago and have started flirting with other women. My gym is the best and the most popular in town; therefore, I don't want to risk having my name on the headlines. Moreover, I have my **late wife**'s brother, James, living in my house. I know for sure that James won't be around tomorrow morning. He is a cop, he leaves on Thursdays and returns on Sundays. As long as I keep it clean, James won't be a problem. I touch the ring on my finger. It reminds me of the love of my life. She was diagnosed with cancer after two years of our marriage. Her memories are still fresh in my mind.

Lydia

"Wow! You mean your sexy boss wants you in his house tomorrow?" Gracie asks. I had told her about Eric.

I turn to Gracie. "Yeah, very early."

"You seem happy about it, Lydia," Gracie winks. "Wait a minute! I hope it's not what I'm thinking? OMG! Lydia, you're in love with your boos?"

I try to hide it from Gracie, but I can't. "I think so."

"You think so?" Now, Gracie is standing close to me with her hand on my shoulder.

"I must admit: I like this guy, but I'm not sure I want to have anything with him."

"Why?"

I scoff. "I feel it's too early. Moreover, he has a ring on his finger. He is married, and I don't want to have anything to do with married men."

"Oh! I see. You should just keep it neutral then."

That is exactly what I am going to do- keep it neutral. I can't afford to mess with my feelings. He is married!

Chapter 3

Lydia

I knock on the door several times, but no answer. There's a doorbell button right beside the door. I press it, and Eric opens.

He is standing right before me with a bare chest and shorts, with a cocky smile on his face. His chest is broad and, of course, sexy. I can't begin to imagine myself on it and planting sweet kisses on it till I get down-

"Please come in," Eric interrupts my thoughts.

I step in. His house is well-furnished and has the most expensive furniture I have ever seen in it. I can see pictures of a woman on the wall. She looks beautiful. I look around and spot a wedding picture on the wall- Eric and his wife.

Eric goes in a room and returns with two tumblers and a bottle of wine in his hands, which he set on the table before me.

"Thank you," I say, as he pours the drink into the cup and hands it over to me.

He finds his way to a chair right in front of me and watches as I sip the fruit wine he had given me.

"So, can we begin?" I ask.

Eric

"I see you're staring at the pictures on the wall."

Since she entered, she has been staring at my wedding photographs and the pictures of my late wife, and I am so sure many questions are running through her mind.

"That's my late wife. She died a month ago. She died of cancer."

"Oh! I never knew that. I'm so sorry," she replies with a look of pity on her face.

"Yeah, it's fine. So, let us begin. Follow me." We both stand up, while I lead us to the workout room.

"So, welcome to my home gym," I say opening my arms wide.

Lydia

I don't know why he invited me over to his house. Seeing the room, I don't think there's any reason to come train him. He has the machines and can work out on his own.

"Can I have those moves you taught those old folks yesterday?"

Really? That will be so simple for him to do. Moreover, it is something he can do all alone.

"Alright," I reply. "Move this way and spread your legs."

I start the moves while he stands behind me watching. I don't think he is doing anything right behind me.

I feel his arms wrap around my waist. Sensations run through my body as I feel the breath from his nostrils landing on my neck. I need him so badly. I can feel something hard right behind my ass: that must be his dick. He begins to suck on my neck while I close my eyes in total enjoyment.

"I knew we would be together the first time I met you. You're such a sexy lady. You torment me. I get jealous at those old men you twist your ass for," he says and fondles my ass with one of his hands. My thighs are beginning to get wet, and I can't wait to feel him.

"It's been eight months since I last had sex, and I need you to recover all that I lost."

I want him to stop the stories and just pounce on me. I know how hard it is for a once-married man to go without sex for a long time, and I want to satisfy his urge and make him feel the sweetness of a woman again.

"I hope you have condoms," I ask him.

"Oh! Yeah." He releases his grip, leaves the room, and returns with a pack of condoms in his hand.

"We are covered, baby."

He grabs my neck and sucks hard on my mouth. One of his hands finds its way to my shirt and unbuttons it. I am now in my bra only. He cups my tits with his hands and begins to fondle them carelessly. I groan at the pleasure that I am beginning to enjoy while his mouth is still fixed on my mouth.

I reach for his shorts and bring out the hard dick. He unbuttons my skirt and uses his fingers to brush my thigh. I groan aloud as he bends and begins to lick every drop of my sweet juice from my tight pussy. We move to the wall close to the window. He sends me completely over the edge when he runs two fingers in and out of my pussy and balances the rest of the fingers on my clit.

"I need you to fuck me hard, boss."

"I like it when you call me boss. It makes me feel like I own you, and I'm going to prove that to you now."

I slide my hand between us and cup his cock, giving it a hard squeeze. I let it go into my pussy slowly while we both moan softly. He begins to ride me hard and fast with his gaze on my eyes.

I moan through my release, not ashamed that he made me come in less than five minutes.

"I've got you, baby," he says and continues to ride without stopping. He groans as he reaches his peak.

We both land on the mat on the floor, panting heavily from our great ride.

"No more training?" I ask.

Eric chuckles. "What we just did is an exercise." He plants a kiss on my forehead.

"I have to go now," I say.

"Really? No, you don't have to go now."

I notice the ring on his finger. "You just cheated on your wife, you know."

He raises his hand to look at the innocent ring sitting on his finger. "I don't think I want to take it off for now."

What he just said creates a little jealousy in me. Eric doesn't want to take the ring off, and he wants to continue having sex with me. *Who does that?*

I jump to my feet and start to get dressed. He remains on the mat staring at me as I get dressed.

"Where are you off to?"

"The Gym"

He let out a cocky smile. "I'm your boss, you know? I decide when you start work and when you close. You're here now, and you're not leaving until afternoon or evening."

"Afternoon or evening?" I ask, surprised. "Yeah. I think I prefer evening."

"As much as you are my boss, I can't stop doing my job." I return to him, kiss his cheeks, and then leave the room.

As I am about to leave his house, I run into a guy about Eric's age. He looks at me and walks into the house without uttering a single word. He looks so strange, and I hate the way he looked at me earlier, like I had come to steal something in the house.

Eric

"Hey man, you're back."

James has entered the room. He didn't tell me he would be coming back today. Today's Tuesday, and he is supposed to be here on Thursday.

"Yeah, I'm here to pick up something," he replies, looking around like there is something strange in the room.

"By the way, who was that?" James asks.

"Oh! The lady that just left? She is one of my employees," I reply, hiding the rest from him.

"And-"

I interrupt. "I asked her to come to give me a personal training this morning."

James let out a grin. "Personal. I see. Alright, I have to return now. I think I know where it is." He leaves the room.

That was so close! I had told James that Lydia is just an employee but didn't tell him about the feelings I have for her. Did I just deny my feelings for her? I touch the ring on my finger again. I have to deal with this once and for all if I claim to love Lydia.

Chapter 4

Lydia

The next day, I rush to work early and start training. It's been two hours, and I have not set eyes on Eric. I am done with the 7:00 a.m. to 8:a.m. training, and the next training starts at 9:00 a.m. Therefore, I have an hour break before the next session. I decide to rest on one of the chairs and watch as students begin to chat with one another. I still haven't seen Eric.

What we had yesterday is nothing to forget. I still want that to happen again. I want Eric again. I need to make him feel I am the best shoulder to cry on. Eric had told me that he is a widow and, honestly, on one hand, I feel so sorry for him, but on the other hand, I am happy that there's no third party. *The ring-* I don't think I want to see the ring with Eric again. I want him to forget about his past and accept the fact that I am the new woman in his life.

I am done for the day, and I have not seen Eric. When I asked the security man, he said he has not seen him today either. Should I just go to his house or pretend like I'm cool with his absence? Since what we had yesterday, we have not spoken to each other- no texts and no calls. *Maybe what we had isn't serious.* I will be heading straight home now and preparing for tomorrow. I carry my bag, sign out, and leave the gym.

Eric

I am at home. I didn't go to work today. I must admit that I miss Lydia so much, and I want to see her again. I had taken a day off to prepare for the rich date with Lydia in two hours in one of the most expensive restaurants here. I haven't told her anything yet, but I am sure she would like to go out with me. I've been praying she doesn't turn me out tonight. I haven't heard anything from her since yesterday- she must have been expecting my call or text. I pick my phone and begin to type.

Eric: Let's meet at 7:00p.m- LIS restaurant. Please reply as soon as you get this message.

I click on the send button as my heart begins to pray she gets the message early and gives me a positive response. She is never going to regret my date with her tonight.

Lydia

I'm home now. My cousin is nowhere to be found. I had called her earlier, and she said she would be back in three to four hours. So, I'm the only one in this house for now. As I walk towards the kitchen to get some chocolates from the refrigerator, my phone beeps with a message. I must go get my apple before I go through the message. That could be Gracie ordering me to do something before she returns. I return to my room with the apple in my hand, pick up my phone, and unlock it. The message is from Eric. *Am I dreaming or something?*

Eric: Let's meet at 7:00p.m- LIS restaurant. Please reply as soon as you get this message.

LIS? LIS is the most expensive and the richest restaurant in town. I have always wished to go there, and my wish is about to be granted by Eric. At last, there's a text from

Eric. I'm just going to reply to his text to let him know I would love to go on a date with him.

Lydia: Alright, I'll be there.

A few seconds after, his message pops up again.

Eric: Thank you, sexy. See you soon! One more thing- I don't mind seeing you in one of those sexy dresses of yours.

I smile at his message, drop my phone, and begin the ultimate search. I pick my sexy pink dress and try it on. No! I don't want this. I have to look so good for Eric tonight. I want him to yearn for more of me. Gracie had told me that my red short dress looks sexy, so I pick it and put it on. Perfect! It looks so good on me, and I can't wait for him to strip me out of it.

Eric

A beautiful lady that catches everyone's attention in the restaurant walks towards me-she is Lydia. I stand to acknowledge her presence as other men in the restaurant watch with envy looks.

"You look stunning, my lady."

"Thank you."

I so much want this lady again. She sits elegantly before me with a smile on her beautiful face. We both order seafood paella and a bottle of wine.

"So, tell me why you were absent at the gym today," she starts.

"For you, my lady," I reply with a grin.

She starts to blush. "Really?"

"Yeah, so how was your day?" I ask, sipping the wine.

"It was boring without you."

I smile knowing quite well that she really missed me. "Lydia, I'm beginning to love you. Ever since I met you, my life has not been the same, and I want to continue seeing you every day of my life. You're my desire."

I haven't let go of the ring on my finger yet. I know I am doing the wrong thing, but all I need is time. I need to give myself much time- I am very careful of what people out there will say. I can't deny my feelings for this young lady before me, but we have to keep whatever is between us a secret.

"Lydia, I love you and-"

She interrupts *"Hush!* Can we get in your car later?"

I am so excited right now. I can feel the excitement of my cock as well as it gets hard.

"I can't wait, baby."

A few minutes later, we head straight to the park hand-in-hand.

I look around to see if anyone is coming, but there's no one- it seems safe. I carry her like a hungry lion with its prey, open the car, and lay her on the back seat.

"No! I'll ride you tonight right on the driver's seat," she says. She leaves the back seat, leads me to the other side of the car, forces the door open, and pushes me in the driver seat. I hurriedly let go of my trousers.

"Oh!" She exclaims at my erected dick. She gets down slowly and begins to suck the hell out of my dick so fast. She swallows every single drop that finds its way into her mouth while I moan softly. *I want this woman so badly. I can't afford to lose her.* She stops sucking my dick. She pulls her dress up so I can see her white lingerie. She smiles seductively as she slowly pulls the panties down her legs. She turns the stereo on and lets soft romantic music play. She sits slowly on my thighs and finds her way to my dick- she begins to ride me from slow to fast as we kiss.

Lydia

I pull down my dress while Eric gets in his trousers.

"Will you be at work tomorrow?" I ask him. Earlier today, I didn't like the fact that he didn't show up at work. I missed every part of him and will not want to miss him again tomorrow.

"Yeah, I should be at work. For you," he smiles and plants a kiss on my neck. "You don't need to call a cab. I'll drive you home."

I laugh. "Don't tell me you're planning to get naughty with me at my place tonight. I have a roommate."

"*Shit!* Your roomie is going to spoil my plans."

"Naughty you." I grin and give him a long kiss.

"You've always wanted to be a trainer?" Eric asks, looking serious now.

"Yes. I also hope to own one someday."

"Wow! That's quite interesting. I mean you're such an uncommon jewel. Don't you see we are cool together? I have a gym, and you are interested in owning one."

I only reply to his question with a smile. "Can you take me home now? We should get going, or I can call a taxi."

"Okay," he sighs while I hop in the car and we head straight to my house.

"Thank you for tonight," he says as he parks right in front of my house.

"Thank you too," I reply while he kisses me on the forehead. I hop out of the car and watch as he drives off.

As I turn to go into the house, I see Gracie standing with her hands on her hips.

"When did you start going on a date without my consent?"

I laugh as I see her confused look.

"It's not funny, you know," she screams.

"I'm sorry. I forgot to call, and I actually thought I would be coming back home early."

"You forgot?" her tone begins to rise.

I move closer to her and give her a tight hug. "I'm sorry, Gracie."

She sighs. "It's fine." She let out a smile to show that she is no longer mad at me. "So, who was that?"

"That was my boss."

"Wow!" she exclaims. "Let's go inside. I want to hear the full gist." She drags me in.

Chapter 5

Lydia

We have been dating for almost a month now, and our love keeps burning day by day. I begin to prepare for today's work. Gracie had left the house early for a school meeting.

As I arrive at the gym, I head straight to Eric's office when I realize that most of my students are not around yet.

"Good morning." I move close to him and kiss him.

"Morning, beauty."

I make myself comfortable on the chair before him. As I am about to bring up a conversation, I hear a knock on the door.

"Yes, please," Eric says, looking towards the door. Steve, Eric's friend, enters while I stand to leave the room.

"See you after training, Lydia," Eric calls out while I nod and leave the office.

Eric

"I see the way you look at that lady," Steve says, jerking me out of my thoughts. "Finally, you're beginning to love again, and I'm happy about that."

I begin to blush.

"I know that face," Steve says, grinning devilishly. I begin to tell Steve my new love story.

After closing hour, Lydia decides to follow me to my house and probably spend the night. Hand-in-hand, we move to my room and begin to kiss- just then I hear the doorbell ring.

"Are you expecting someone?" Lydia asks, buttoning the shirt she has started to unbutton a few minutes ago.

I am not expecting anyone and today's Tuesday. James can't be home this time.

"I'm not expecting anyone. Hold on, let me check." I leave the room and slam the door to see who the person is- who is trying to deprive me of fun?

I open the door and alas! James is standing with a bag in his hand.

"Hi, there's nothing to do at work this week. I'm on break, so I'm just going to spend it here till maybe next Thursday," James says with a wide smile on his face as he finds his way in, leaving me at the entrance. James and I don't talk that much because he is always busy at work; therefore, I didn't get to tell him about Lydia. It seems too late to start talking about her now, especially when she is right in the house- in my bedroom. I close the door slowly and return to my room.

"Hey, who was that?" Lydia whispers. I haven't told her about James yet, my late wife's brother, because I thought it didn't matter.

"My late wife's brother. We live here together," I reply, avoiding her eyes.

Lydia

"You live together? How come you never told me this? How come this is just getting to me?" I ask angrily. Eric has never once mentioned James until now. I'm freaking out right now. I begin to pace up and down the room. How am I supposed to leave the house? How am I supposed to leave his room right before James' face? *For goodness sake!* He is his late wife's brother- she died only a month ago, and I am here in his house.

"You planned to stay the night, didn't you?" Eric asks.

"Yeah, but I don't think I want to stay any longer. I need to go home. I can't remain here. I can't sleep over," I reply grabbing my bag from the bed.

"Are you sure about this?" he asks, looking at me confusingly. I nod my head. He holds my hand confidently and leads me out. I am so fortunate- James isn't outside, so I elegantly walk out of the house with Eric, who decides to drop me off.

Lydia

Two days later as I get to work, the strange man I had seen at Eric's place is sitting patiently in the gym with his legs crossed and his arms folded. I pretend like I didn't see him as I go on with today's work. After the first session, I hear a voice right behind me. "Hello, I am James Brown, and I'm Eric's brother-in-law."

OMG! "Okay." I forced a fake smile. "Mr. Martins should be in his office."

"No, I am here to see you, not Eric."

My heart begins to beat faster. "Okay. How may I help you?" I ask confidently as I lead us to sit in a corner.

"Once again, I'm James Brown, Eric's in-law. I'm also a cop. My sister died about two months ago. I really loved her. Eric loved her too. She died of cancer. Let me just get straight to the point. I would like you to leave Eric alone, so as to save your precious time. Eric still loves my sister. He even has the ring on his finger. Can't you see he is not ready to let go of my sister? If he truly loves you, he should deal with that ring and prove his love to you."

He pauses for a minute and continues. "Please, don't get it wrong. I am not here to hurt how you feel about Eric, but you need to understand that he doesn't love you. He loves his late wife." As soon as he is done, he stands up, stretches forth his hand for a handshake, which I receive slowly. He leaves the gym, leaving me perplexed on the chair. He said the truth. I have to wake up from my dreams after having sex with Eric four times.

Eric

I notice Lydia has been avoiding me these days. She no longer comes to my office and turns to leave whenever I approach her. These days, she has been so serious with her work here and pretends I am not in the gym. She has not been picking my calls and replying to my texts. If what she wants is to keep avoiding me without a reason, I'm just going to let her be- but I do love her and do not pray for this solitude to last longer.

Lydia

A few weeks after…

"You're pregnant!" Gracie cries out loud.

This can't be happening. I have tried five pregnancy test kits now, and I got the same result from each of them. I have gone so careless, and I feel so bad right now. When did this happen?- *oh!* I remember there was no condom the night we had sex in his car. *Shit! Not when I'm planning to leave town.* I made up my mind a week ago to travel out of town to spend a whole month with my dad. Since James told me about Eric and the feelings Eric still has for his late wife, I have been so devastated.

I tried avoiding Eric and focusing on my work, but I can no longer continue. Eric doesn't want to let go of his wife, and he wants to keep messing around with me. I love him, but I don't think he is ready to let go of his wife for me. I have been feeling sick these days and decided to get the pregnancy test kits earlier when Gracie suggested I did.

"So, are you still leaving?" Gracie asks almost in a whispery voice.

I nod. "Yeah. My plan hasn't changed."

She exclaims. "What! Even with the fetus growing in your womb?" She begins to pace up and down the room with her hand on her forehead. "But how could you be so careless, Lydia? Aren't you on pills?"

"I'm not. I admit I was so careless. I stopped using pills two months ago or thereabout." I burst into tears. "I'm just going to leave town. Eric doesn't want to admit that he loves me. His heart belongs to his late wife and not me. I'll take care of this baby."

Gracie turns to leave for her room but stops abruptly. "Wait! How do you know he doesn't love you? I think he is just being careful."

Careful? I scoff at that word. Nothing is going to stop me from leaving. My flight is in 48 hours.

Eric

Lydia had come to my office a few days ago with a resignation letter. We didn't say anything to each other. Since she gave me the resignation letter, I haven't been myself. I stop going to work and decide to stay at home-indoors.

In her resignation letter, she had said her reason for resigning is because she wants to go start her own gym in another town. That didn't sound true to me.

"Hey man," James says as he enters the house. "You look sick."

"I'm fine," I lie to him. I am not fine at all.

There is a long silence in the room before James breaks it. "Eric. You never told me about the lady that came here a few weeks ago."

My heart skips a beat.

James continues, "I saw her leaving the house that night. I peeped through my door. Anyways, that's no longer a problem. I think I already did you two a favor."

I begin to get confused. What exactly is he talking about?

"I don't understand you," I say, adjusting myself on the seat.

"That was your employee. I told her everything about the love you have for my sister. You've not gotten rid of my sister's memory. I told her you still love my sister and not her."

"What!" I exclaim angrily.

"The ring! You still have the ring on your finger. That shows you are not certain of the love you have for her. If you really are, this ring wouldn't be on your finger," James says with a big frown on his face. "You can't claim to love her and keep that ring on your finger. Moreover, my sister died just a few months ago and-"

I interrupt him. "You think I am ashamed of the love I have for my employee? I'm not. As a matter of fact, I'll deal with this ring right now." I pause. "James, I can't hide anymore. I love Lydia so much. You know quite well that, if your sister were alive, I wouldn't cheat on her. I loved your sister so much." I force the ring off my finger and let it go into the trash basket.

James sighs deeply. "Then you have to go for her if you really do love her." He moves close me to and pats me on the back. "You can do this, man. Go for your love."

Epilogue

Eric

"Hurry! Hurry!!" James and Gracie yell as we ride fast in my car. James and I had gone to Lydia's house early this morning, but she was not around. Gracie told me that Lydia is about leaving town today, and she must be at the airport by now. She also told me about the pregnancy. I have to stop Lydia. She can't leave just like that. I'll be so miserable if she does.

I drive as fast as I can and park right in front of the airport while we all run to the lounge. We look around to see if Lydia is there, but there's no sign of her.

"No! Lydia can't be gone," I say, looking worried. There are so many people in the lounge, but spotting Lydia in the midst of thousands isn't difficult for me. I walk towards one of the attendants.

"Hey!"

"Wow! It's nice seeing you, Mr. Martins, the owner of the biggest gym in town. I'm a big fan of yours," the female attendant says happily with a big grin on her face.

"Thank you," I reply and force a smile out.

"How may I help you, sir?"

"Please, when did the last plane leave?" I ask hurriedly.

"Twenty minutes ago. You just missed your flight?"

"No! Please, I need you to check if there's any Lydia Staples on that plane," I say while she opens the book before her to check. She nods her head after searching.

"There's no Lydia Staples on the last plane. She will be leaving in the next plane."

"Thank you."

I sigh with relief as I return to James and Gracie.

"Oh! There she is!" Gracie screams, pointing towards the entrance of the lounge. Lydia walks in while we rush towards her.

"Eric?" she asks, surprised. "What are you doing here?" She begins to smile happily. I go down on my knees right in front of the crowd and bring out the little box in my pocket. The whole lounge goes silent.

"I want to spend the rest of my life with you. I want this baby growing in your womb. I'm going to love you both unconditionally. I don't care what people say because I so much love you. I don't want to hide you anymore. I don't want to hide us. All that matters now is you. Please marry me."

I see tears rolling down her cheeks with a smile on her face as she nods and stretches her fingers forward for me to fit the ring in place. There are cheers and claps everywhere as Lydia accepts my proposal. She cancels the flight, and we all leave the airport.

I help the love of my life achieve her dreams by building her a gym twice bigger than mine. I can never be this happy without her.

www.ingramcontent.com/pod-product-compliance
Lightning Source LLC
Chambersburg PA
CBHW030413160726
47992CB00007B/3095